SKYLARK CHOOSE YOUR OWN ADVENTURE® • 2

READ THIS FIRST!!!

Most books are about other people.
This book is about you!
What happens to you in the haunted house depends on what you decide to do.
Do not read this book from the first page through to the last page.

Instead, start at page one and read until you come to your first choice. Then turn to the page shown and see what happens.

When you come to the end of a story, go back and try another choice. every choice leads to a new adventure.

Good luck!

THE HAUNTED HOUSE

R. A. MONTGOMERY

ILLUSTRATED BY PAUL GRANGER

A BANTAM SKYLARK BOOK®
TORONTO · NEW YORK · LONDON · SYDNEY

RL 2, 007-009

THE HAUNTED HOUSE
A Bantam Skylark Book / November 1981
2nd printing . . . November 1981   4th printing . . . . . February 1982
3rd printing . . . December 1981   5th printing . . . . July 1982

CHOOSE YOUR OWN ADVENTURE ® is a
trademark of Bantam Books, Inc.

Skylark Books is a registered trademark of Bantam Books, Inc.,
Registered in the U.S. Patent Office and elsewhere.

Illustrated by Paul Granger

ISBN 0-553-15119-3

Published simultaneously in the United States and Canada

Bantam Books are published by Bantam Books, Inc. Its trade-
mark, consisting of the words "Bantam Books" and the por-
trayal of a rooster, is Registered in U.S. Patent and Trademark
Office and in other countries. Marca Registrada. Bantam
Books, Inc., 666 Fifth Avenue, New York, New York 10103.

PRINTED IN THE UNITED STATES OF AMERICA

C   14   13   12   11   10   9   8   7

This book
is dedicated to
Anson,
Ramsey,
and
Judy

You and your dog Homer are walking home from school for lunch one day. Since he loves to play, you pick up a stick from the sidewalk and give it a big toss. Homer goes after it.

Suddenly a white cat runs in front of him and—zoom!—Homer starts chasing the cat. Homer chases her right into the yard of a big grey house. But you stop short at the gate.

Wow! It looks as if nobody has lived here for years. The grass is uncut. The front door is slightly open. Most of the windows are broken, and there are shingles missing from the roof. It's definitely a scary-looking old house. Maybe it's haunted!

Homer is nowhere in sight. You call out for him.

"Homer! Hey, Homer! Come back, Homer."

NO ANSWER.

Turn to page 2.

2   You *have* to find Homer. He's your friend. You enter the front yard through the old, rusty gate. You tiptoe around to the back of the house. You see a stone bench and an empty fish pond, but no Homer.

You sit down on the bench to think for a minute. Even though it's warm out, the stone bench makes you feel very cold. All of a sudden there is an icy gust of wind. You are freezing! You hear a voice *coming from inside the house!*

"HOMER IS IN THE HOUSE."

The voice is deep and loud, and very, very scary. You want to find Homer, but that voice is so awful that you don't want to go near the house. What should you do?

If you go into the house, turn to page 9.

If you run away, turn to page 5.

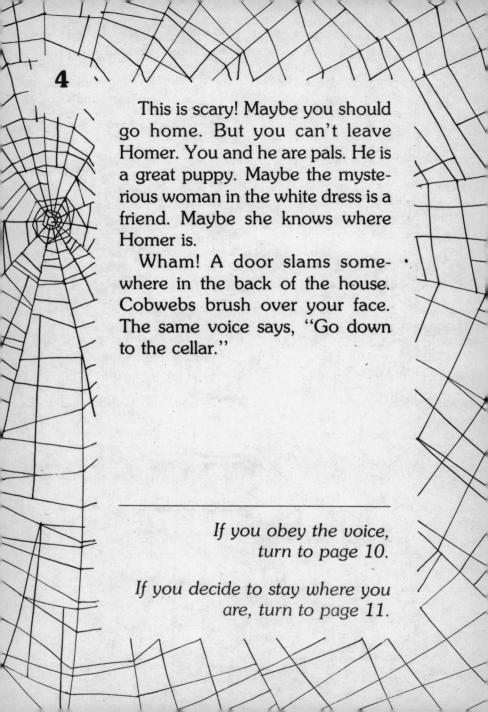

This is scary! Maybe you should go home. But you can't leave Homer. You and he are pals. He is a great puppy. Maybe the mysterious woman in the white dress is a friend. Maybe she knows where Homer is.

Wham! A door slams somewhere in the back of the house. Cobwebs brush over your face. The same voice says, "Go down to the cellar."

If you obey the voice, turn to page 10.

If you decide to stay where you are, turn to page 11.

You run faster than you've ever run be- **5**
fore. Suddenly you fall down some stairs.

BUMP
BUMP
KA-BUMP

You are knocked out. You see stars. When
you wake up, you are *inside the house!* It is
very dark and dusty. You are terrified!

If you scream for help, turn to page 12.

If you stay quiet and wait, turn to page 13.

You follow the mysterious woman outside. You can jump a mile high! You can even fly! You are having so much fun that you nearly forget about Homer!

If you continue on with the woman, turn to page 16.

If you want to find Homer, turn to page 17.

The crocodile crawls toward you and snaps again. It catches you by the shirt. The shirt rips. The crocodile grabs you by the sneaker. It pulls you into the water. Ughhh!

It's funny, though—the crocodile's teeth are not sharp. They feel like rubber teeth. And the water is warm and comfortable.

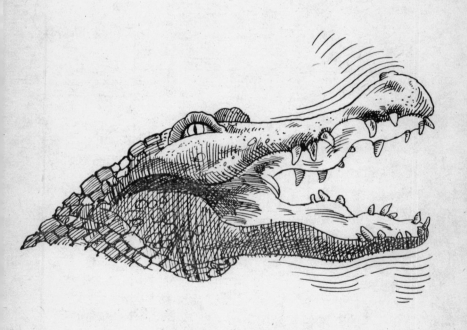

Turn to page 33.

"After all," you say to yourself, "this is just an empty house. It's not really haunted." So you decide to go in through the boarded-up back door.

You pull a board aside and push the door open. Creak!! It is damp inside and smells like an old sneaker. You tiptoe into the dark room, holding your breath so you won't make any noise. Suddenly a woman in a white dress appears. She smiles at you and disappears into the darkness.

If you try to follow the mysterious woman, turn to page 6.

If you're not sure what to do, turn to page 4.

10 It's creepy going down into the cellar.

A bat swoops low. Rats scurry about. A river runs through the cellar! There is a blue boat tied to a metal ring in the wall.

If you get into the boat, turn to page 18.

If you walk along the bank, turn to page 19.

You stay where you are. A trap door **11**
swings open. You climb down the rickety
ladder and find yourself in a bright room.
The room is filled with mirrors that make you
look very, very tall, or very, very fat, or very,
very skinny.

Turn to page 40.

You hear the thump, thump of your own heart. You feel so alone that you begin to yell. A bat flies by. He is as big as you are! He says, "I'll help you. Just climb on my back."

It might be useful to have this bat as a friend.

If you fly with the bat, turn to page 20.

If you hide from the bat, turn to page 22.

Time doesn't seem to move. The darkness **13**
gets even darker. You are too terrified to
breathe. You want to go home.

Then it happens. A furry thing touches
your hand.

Ick! Yuck! What is it? Could it be Homer?

If you want to find out, turn to page 23.

*If you don't want to find out,
turn to page 24.*

14 "OK, Mr. Mouse, lead the way."

He grins at you. His nose twitches in a cheerful way like a rabbit's. The two of you push aside a blue curtain and go down a flight of stairs. The mouse shows you two keys. One is gold and the other is silver.

There are two doors in front of you. They are made of wood and have big locks. One lock is silver and the other is gold.

The mouse holds out the two keys and says, "Go ahead. You choose."

If you take the golden key, turn to page 41.

If you take the silver key, turn to page 42.

16   You follow the mysterious woman higher and higher. Soon she stops on a cloud. Sun shines right through her. She smiles at you. Then she walks up a sunbeam.

You follow her. When you look back, the scary house is just a little grey dot.

Maybe it's time to turn around.

If you do turn back and leave the mysterious woman, turn to page 26.

If you want to see where the sunbeam takes you, turn to page 29.

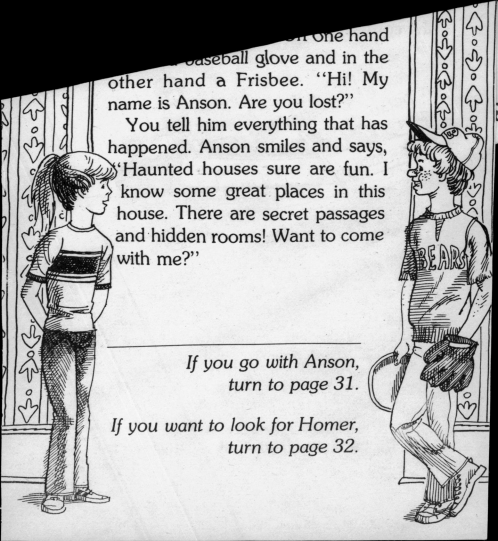

One hand ...baseball glove and in the other hand a Frisbee. "Hi! My name is Anson. Are you lost?"

You tell him everything that has happened. Anson smiles and says, "Haunted houses sure are fun. I know some great places in this house. There are secret passages and hidden rooms! Want to come with me?"

*If you go with Anson,
turn to page 31.*

*If you want to look for Homer,
turn to page 32.*

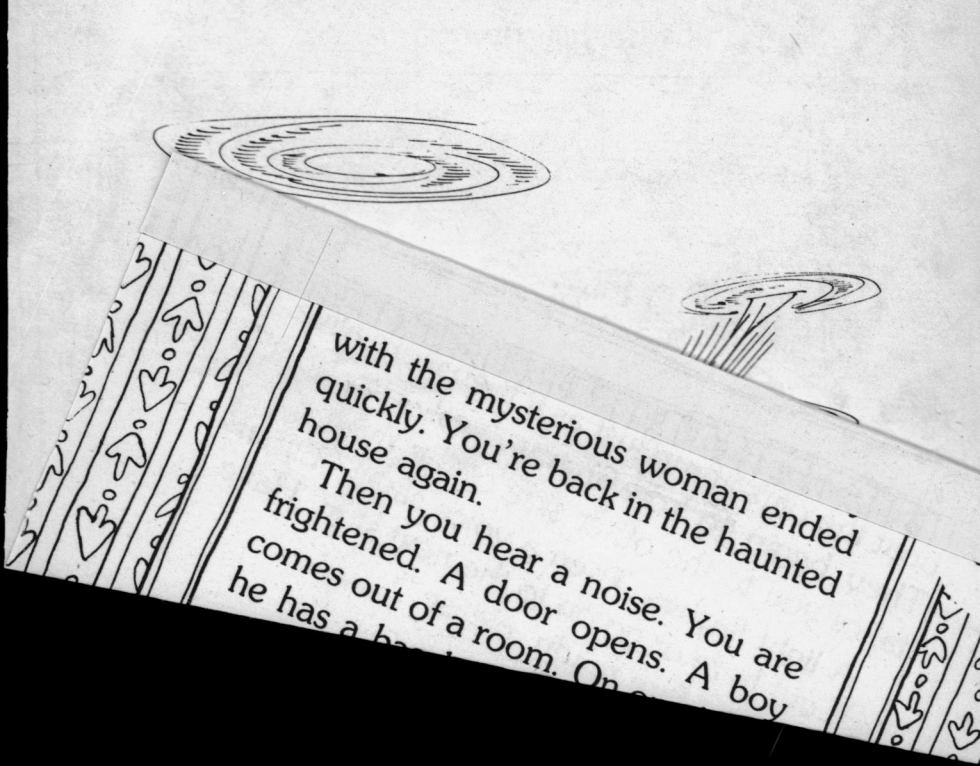

with the mysterious woman ended quickly. You're back in the haunted house again.

Then you hear a noise. You are frightened. A door opens. A boy comes out of a room. On ... he has a ba...

If you get out, turn to page 36.

If you stay in the boat, turn to page 37.

You decide that it's safer on land than it is in the boat. But at least you can walk wherever you want.

You start walking down the bank of the river. It is muddy and gluppy. Suddenly two red eyes stare out at you from the water.

Snap!

It's a crocodile. You jump back and hit the rocky wall of the tunnel. You are just far enough away from the crocodile to be safe.

Turn to page 7.

20   The bat spreads his wings and his eyes twinkle. You climb up onto his back. You fly through a window out of the house and high up into the sky. You land in a garden. Big pieces of fruit cover the ground. The apples are red and yellow, and they're as big as cars. The pears are bigger than trucks!

You relax and take a huge bite out of a giant pear. You get soaked in pear juice. Ick! It's sticky.

You lie out in the sun to dry off a bit, and then you decide to go exploring.

Turn to page 46.

22   You decide you don't really want to go off with the bat. Instead you hide in a dark room under a pile of old blankets and clothing. It's warm and comfortable. Soon you fall asleep.

When you wake up, you hear a noise. It sounds like thunder. The noise gets louder and louder. You see light under the door to the room. You open the door a crack.

Turn to page 48.

24 You certainly don't want to know what the furry thing is! You run up the stairs and go into a little room. Sun shines through a broken window. You see two kids. They smile at you, and one says, "Hi! Where did you come from?"

You tell them you came from downstairs!

Turn to page 52.

26   You can't turn back. You've climbed so far on the sunbeam that now you are part of the sunbeam. You sparkle and you shine, and you help light the world.

The End

You leave the mouse and run down the tunnel alone. The tunnel leads into a room with two doors. One door is yellow and very big. The other is red and very small.

If you go through the yellow door, turn to page 45.

If you go through the red door, turn to page 38.

You climb the sunbeam. The steps are **29**
made of gold, and they are just the right size
for you.

The air is warm and smells good. You hear
music playing. It sounds familiar, but you
can't quite tell what the song is. It is so
pleasant up on the sunbeam that you want to
go on walking forever.

Hold on! Shouldn't you turn back now?
After all, what about Homer, and home, and
school, and your friends?

If you turn back, turn to page 54.

If you continue, turn to page 56.

The mouse
looks friendly, but
you're not fooled. You
are better off finding
Homer on your own.
The ladder is steep and hard
to climb. As you climb, you
hear the sound of wind above
you. The wind rushes down the
trap door, picks you up, and
carries you upward.
You spin in a white cloud.

Turn to page 34.

Anson leads you into a big room.

Surprise!! It's your birthday, and this is your party. All your friends gather around you. Your mom is holding the biggest chocolate cake you've ever seen. Homer is sitting at the head of the table. He looks ready to blow out the candles. Beat him to it!

The End

32   "I'd love to go with you, but I have to find my dog," you tell Anson.

"I think I know where Homer is."

Anson leads you to a door on the second floor. There is a big sign that says,

ADMISSION 25¢

Anson pays for both of you. Wow! It's a movie about Superman. The place is jammed. And there is Homer sitting in the front row. There are two empty seats right next to him. Homer has saved them for you and Anson! He even brought you popcorn.

You settle back and enjoy the movie. What a great day you've had.

The End

You stick your finger into the crocodile's eye. "Yikes! That's not fair," he screams. He lets go. You swim to shore and run along the bank. The crocodile climbs up the bank and follows you, crying. "I wasn't going to hurt you. I just wanted to play."

A path on the river bank leads outside. You are free. Homer is there. He licks your face. You won't go back to this old house. Not on your life!

The End

The cloud is soft, fluffy, and comfortable. Soon the wind dies down, and it is quiet. You float over the earth in your cloud-bed.

All of a sudden you are wet. It's raining! The cloud gets smaller and smaller and you fall out. You ride the gentle rain back down to the haunted house.

Go on to the next page.

What a trip! You hope you can remember everything that has happened. You can't wait to get home.

Homer runs up and licks your face. Ugh! Yucky dog lips!

The End

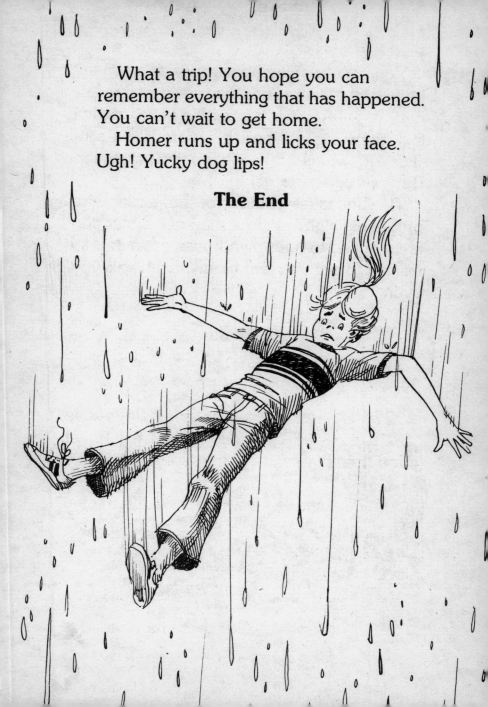

36 You get out of the boat and walk down the bank of the river. Then you see a pretty garden. Wow! Right in the middle of the garden is a funny-looking bus. It's more like a sausage on wheels. There's no driver, either. But you decide to get in.

The bus takes you out of the garden and onto a big highway. In a snap of a finger you are whizzed to your own house. Homer is so excited to see you that he nearly knocks you over.

The End

You give the boat conductor fifty cents. **37**
The boat has wings. You can actually fly it.
You fly up to the sky and over the land. Right
below you is your own house. Your mother
is in the back yard. She waves at you. You
land the boat in the yard.

"Welcome home," she says as she hugs
you.

The End

38 You're in luck! The red door opens into a circus. You see your brother there. He is having a great time. You join a group of

clowns. You're in an act where you all get into a mini-car. No one can believe it when 14 of you clowns get out of the tiny red car.

The End

40   There is a tunnel at one end of the room. A fat brown mouse appears at the end of the tunnel. He says, "Don't be scared. I'm your friend. Follow me and we'll have fun."

If you follow the mouse down the tunnel, turn to page 14.

If you run by him and go down the tunnel alone, turn to page 27.

If you go back up the ladder, turn to page 30.

Hurray for you! Good choice!

You chose the golden key and the door to safety. Homer runs up, wagging his tail. The tunnel ends in your own back yard!

The End

The silver key is magic. When you hold it, you can fly up to the top of the tallest mountain in the world. You can see for hundreds of miles! Finally you return to earth and your own home. Homer is in the front yard. He wags his tail, jumps up and gives you a big, wet, sloppy kiss.

The End

"Who are you?"

"Well, you see, I am the mayor of this town. And I ask the same of you. Who, just who, are you to be eating our houses?"

You tell him your name.

He bows and shakes your hand.

"How do I get home from here?" you ask.

He says, "Just wish it, and you'll be there."

You close your eyes and wish and—poof!—you are home.

The End

Surprise! The yellow door opens onto the **45** baseball field behind your school. You are in center field, and a ball is coming right at you.

You look up just in time and catch the baseball in your bare hands. All the kids yell, "Hurray! We win!"

Your teammates surround you and give you big hugs. You saved the game.

All the rest was a daydream you had while standing in center field. You can't wait to get home to see Homer.

The End

Amazing! You come upon
a house made of cream puffs.
Next to the cream puff house is
one made up of éclairs. You take a
taste of both houses. You stroll down the
street. Everywhere you see houses made

of your favorite desserts. What a great place! **47**
    Then you hear a voice. It says, "Hey, don't eat my house, I live in it." When you look around you see a small, strange man no bigger than a cat.

Turn to page 43.

48

Go on to page 49.

Wake up! Fireworks. You look out your **49**
bedroom window. There are four kids setting
off firecrackers.

Of course! It's the Fourth of July.

You go back to sleep, wondering what you
will dream next.

The End

You made a big, big mistake. The candy turns you into a furry turtle. Too bad.

The End

Good for you! You didn't know the turtle. You never know what could have been in those candies. The turtle eats the candy and turns into a rock.

You step over the rock and find a secret door in the wall. The door leads to the side yard of the house near the big trees. The sun shines on you. You are safe. And there is Homer, bringing you the stick that led you to your adventure in the haunted house.

The End

52 "I don't want to go any further. I'm scared."

"OK. Follow us." The two kids lead you to a secret staircase. It is dark and dusty. The climb up the stairs seems endless.

Then suddenly you are out on a porch. There is a rope ladder on the railing. You drop the ladder to the ground and climb down.

"Yip! Yip! Yip!" It is Homer. He is waiting for you outside. He is safe and so are you.

You wave goodbye to your friends. When you turn back you see Homer chasing after another white cat.

Oh, no!

The End

54 The sunbeam turns into a giant slide.
Whooooosh!
You end up in the funhouse
at the amusement park.

The End

You decide to continue following the mysterious woman. At last she turns right and stops.

"There is the path to Venus. Follow it if you wish." Then she vanishes—poof!—in a puff of pink smoke.

You start to walk on the path. It is beautiful. Venus seems very small. Venus has windows and curtains and wallpaper and swimming trophies and—wait! It's your own room!

You sit up in bed. It was all a dream.

The End

ABOUT THE AUTHOR

R. A. MONTGOMERY is an educator and publisher. A graduate of Williams College, he also studied in graduate programs at Yale University and New York University. After serving in a variety of administrative capacities at Williston Academy and Columbia University, he co-founded the Waitsfield Summer School in 1965. Following that, Montgomery helped found a research and development firm specializing in the development of educational programs. He worked for several years as a consultant to the Peace Corps in Washington, D.C. and West Africa. For the last five years, he has been both a writer and a publisher.

ABOUT THE ILLUSTRATOR

PAUL GRANGER is a prize-winning illustrator and painter.